Snore All Sunday!

and Other Stories

Arthy Muthanna Singh

Ukiyoto Publishing

All global publishing rights are held by

Ukiyoto Publishing

Published in 2025

Content Copyright © *Arthy Muthanna Singh*
ISBN 9789370093546

All rights reserved.

No part of this publication may be reproduced, transmitted, or stored in a retrieval system, in any form by any means, electronic, mechanical, photocopying, recording or otherwise, without the prior permission of the publisher.

The moral rights of the author have been asserted.

This book is sold subject to the condition that it shall not by way of trade or otherwise, be lent, resold, hired out or otherwise circulated, without the publisher's prior consent, in any form of binding or cover other than that in which it is published.

www.ukiyoto.com

Dedication

I dedicate this book to my son, who turned out to be a voracious reader too!

Contents

SNORE ALL SUNDAY!	1
THE MYSTERIOUS VOICE!	4
A ZERO CAN BE A HERO TOO!	8
CAN I GO TO THE CIRCUS?	12
PINKY PANTHER'S PIMPLE PROBLEM	15
GRANDPA, YOU LOOK LIKE A BEET ROOT!	20
MONKEY TRICKS!	22
THE PAVEMENT CLUB	24
THE SUN'S ON STRIKE!	26
THE BORED SCARECROW!	29
RAMAN'S DREAM	33
A PASSENGER WITHOUT A TICKET!	35
About the Author	*39*

SNORE ALL SUNDAY!

Yes, that is exactly what Natasha's dad would love to do! But do you think Natasha and her brother Neil let him? No way! Sunday is their day with their dad, with pillow fights in the morning and soccer in the evening. With a little bit of gardening in the afternoon and maybe, just maybe, a little help from him with their homework too. Natasha's father did not know this, but every Saturday his two children would plan and plot on how they would try to keep their dad awake through Sunday. But every Sunday their father did try to sleep whenever he could and wherever he could. One Sunday in winter, Neil had found Mr.George fast asleep under the divan in the guest bedroom!

"I'm sure he falls asleep in the middle of his important meetings too," he whispered to Natasha as they tried to wake him up. The children had started calling their father Mr George as a joke, ever since a driver from the office had arrived at their home many years ago with a huge file for `Mr George'.

On this particular Sunday during the spring semester, Natasha and Neil had a lot planned to stop their father from sleeping. Their mother was going to be gone all day for a surprise party for her school friend. The children had already soaked some green gram in water on Saturday night so that they could make a salad with the help of their father. And the table in the front porch had all the items required to complete Neil's project that had to be handed in on Monday. He had asked if he could get help from his father and his teacher had said, "Sure." He had to make a pirate paper plate puppet for the play that his class was going to put up on Parents Day at the end of the month.

So, on Sunday morning, as soon as their mother left at 8 am, Natasha and Neil crept into their parents' bedroom to get their father out of bed. First they started with the tickling. When that did not work, they pulled off the bed covers. Their father just snored on! Then Natasha filled her mother's spray can that she used to water the plants with cold water, and sprayed it on her father's face. That worked.

"Okay, okay," Mr George said sleepily, "Please let me sleep for just 5 minutes more."

"No!" shouted Neil and Natasha, as they dragged their father out of bed. Once he was out of bed, they pushed him into the bathroom to get ready. They waited outside patiently. After 15 minutes, when Mr George did not come out, Neil got worried.

"Do you think he has fallen asleep in there?"

Natasha knocked hard on the door, which promptly opened with their father all ready and looking fresh.

"Let's go!" he said, as he walked with his kids to the kitchen. He helped them to make a salad with the green gram that they had soaked.

"Salad for breakfast?" he exclaimed. "Good and healthy!"

The three moved to the porch and after a lot of messy mistakes, Neil's paper plate puppet was finally ready. Natasha made one for herself too.

"Mr George is the Vice President in the office, but he sure doesn't know much about glue!" whispered Natasha as they quickly cleared up the mess before their mother came back.

Paper plate pirate puppet:

What you need:

2 paper plates

stapler or tape

wool, thick paper

glue

felt pens, colour pencils or crayons

1.　　Staple or tape the two plates in such a way so that the bottom of both the plates is on the outside. Leave a gap wide enough for your hand to pass through.

2.　　Make sure that the gap is at the bottom before you paint a face. Use the felt pens to draw the nose, eyes, etc. Stick card paper for an eye patch and wool for hair. Pirate ready!

THE MYSTERIOUS VOICE!

"Wake up, Lazybones, wake up!"

Arjun almost jumped out of his skin. He looked at the clock. It was only 6'o'clock. He still had a full hour before he had to get out of bed. So, who was screaming the place down? It seemed as if someone was shouting outside his window.

"Can't you hear me? Wake up!"

Arjun quickly ran up to the window and drew the curtains apart. No one in sight! Arjun wondered if Akhil, his neighbor, was playing some kind of trick. If he was, his voice sure sounded weird. Arjun had a good look around the garden, but when he could not spot anyone, he decided to try and go back to sleep. Arjun hated getting up early.

He dozed off, deciding to call Akhil as soon as he woke up. But when he did wake up, he had no time to think of Akhil or that voice; he was late. Scrambling out of bed, Arjun rushed through all his chores, leaving the brushing of his teeth for the end. As he squeezed toothpaste onto his brush, he glanced at his watch to find that he had managed to make up for the time he had overslept. Whew! He could brush his teeth leisurely.

"This is the way to brush your teeth, brush your teeth, brush your teeth,

This is the way to brush your teeth, early in the morning."

It was that strange voice again! In the bathroom? What was going on? Arjun was quite perplexed by now. He peered out of the bathroom window, but as he expected, there was nobody there.

`I'll deal with this mystery when I get back from school,' he thought, as he rushed downstairs for breakfast.

At the bus-stop, Arjun found Akhil reading a book.

"Nice trick, Akhil," he said, thumping him on the back.

Akhil looked blank. "What are you talking about?"

"I like the way you disguised your voice," Arjun went on, "Did you use a mike?"

Akhil stared at him in surprise, then rolled his eyes skywards and went back to reading his book.

Arjun suspected that Akhil was pretending to be ignorant, but there was no way he could be sure. Anyway, the school bus arrived and the rest of the day was a busy whirl.

After Arjun got home in the evening, he kept expecting to hear the strange voice, but he did not. By the time he went to bed, he actually wondered if it had all been a dream.

The next morning, Arjun awoke early, half-expecting a few shouts. But it was only when he was brushing his teeth that the irritating voice startled him again .

"I don't think you are feeling well. See a doctor, see a doctor."

Arjun rushed to the bathroom window. Nobody in sight. At the bus stop, Akhil was waiting for him.

"What were you blabbering about yesterday?" he asked. "I thought you had gone nuts."

Arjun hesitated. If he told Akhil and Akhil told anyone else, everyone in his class would laugh at him, but he did want to talk to someone about that strange voice. So he did.

"But please don't tell anyone until we get to the bottom of this mystery. Please."

Akhil nodded. "We'll do a thorough check-up when we get back this evening."

Arjun reached home earlier than Akhil did that evening as he had play practice. Akhil rushed in later.

"Have a look at this," he said as he handed Arjun a newspaper. Someone had put in an advertisement. This is what it said:

`LOST. A beautiful parakeet has been lost since 2.10.2014. The parakeet answers to the name Doc. Doc can talk a little. Please be careful. Doc is sometimes violent towards strangers. If anyone sees Doc, please call 022 – 20224577. Suitable reward guaranteed.'

"That was two days ago. Come on, let's go," said Arjun.

The two boys raced upstairs to Arjun's room. Arjun put his finger to his lips and the boys tip-toed up to the bedroom window. They looked all over but it was only when Akhil climbed onto the window ledge that he finally spotted a beautiful parakeet, fast asleep on the top platform of the window, almost out of sight.

"Bingo!" he whispered to Arjun. "Go call that number. The culprit's sleeping up there!"

ZERO CAN BE A HERO TOO!

Aero liked to behave like a hero. He always wanted to climb the tallest tree and be the first to swim across the river near his home when the children in the neighborhood had a race. And most of all he loved to race his bicycle down the slope of his street so fast that he would be shaking by the time he reached the bottom of the slope!

Aero also wanted to fly. But he never told anyone that. He knew that they would laugh at him. Aero felt like laughing at himself sometimes, but every time he saw a Bulbul on his fence, or a Kingfisher dive through the sir to catch a fish in the river, he would wish, ` If only I could fly.'

Aero's good friend Zero lived down the street, just five houses away. He was a quiet boy who loved to read. But even more than that, he loved to dream; daydream! He would dream about the waves splashing on his feet on Colva Beach in Goa, he dreamed about licking the snowflakes to find out what they tasted like in Ladakh, he dreamed of rolling over and over again on the sand dunes of the Kahahari Desert…it all seemed so real. Oh yes, Zero was a great dreamer!

His mother had hoped that the active Aero would take Zero out to play more often, but Zero preferred to lie on the floor of the verandah with his head upon his favourite cushion and dream.

Life went on as normal in that sleepy town of Menaspur until one fine day, when Aero just decided that he simply had to fly!

He wanted to tell Zero about his wish. Maybe he would be able to help him, he thought.

'He reads so many books. I bet he'll know something about the art of flying. I'll make him promise not to tell anyone.'

When he reached Zero's house, he was dreaming as usual. He was far away inside a speeding metro train in Paris.

"What a wonderful way to mooooove!" he murmured. "Right under the city!"

"Hey Zero!" he heard somebody shout. "What is right under the city?"

Zero opened his eyes to find Aero peering at him.

"The metro. In Paris," replied Zero. "I was thinking about…"

"We could fly to Paris!" interrupted Aero.

"What?" exclaimed Zero, looking fazed.

"I have the most wonderful wish, Zero," whispered Aero. "But you have to help me to make it come true. I must fly!"

Zero gaped at Aero, mouth open wide!

"You are going to help me, right?" begged Aero. "Please Zero. You have to!"

"But how can you fly?" asked Zero. "I don't know how to help you."

He then saw Aero's face fall in disappointment and he added quickly, "But I'll try."

The two friends raced into Zero's room to plan this exciting adventure! Zero drew a lot of diagrams and took out a lot of books from his collection to refer to, while Aero walked around, getting more and more excited!

Days flew by. The friends met every single day now. More plans, more diagrams, more excitement!

'I knew it was a good idea to tell Zero about my wish,' thought Aero happily.

"Okay, let's go to the garage," Zero finally said one Sunday afternoon. He had a strange-looking contraption in his hand, not larger than a novel.

In the garage, Zero pulled out his father's old musty parachute. His father had been a helicopter pilot in the Air Force years ago. His mother had forgotten to throw it out.

A large, cane picnic basket came out next, along with a tool-kit, rope, hooks, nuts and bolts, etc.

"Come on and help me," he called.

Ropes were tied, hooks were installed, bolts were tightened and Zero's contraption was put in place, with Zero constantly referring to his strange-looking diagrams. It was late evening by the time they were done.

"We'll need to go up to the terrace to test this," said Zero.

The funny-looking thing that they had made was carefully carried up to the terrace.

"I'm going to fly! I'm going to fly! I'm really going to FLY!" shouted Aero, at the top of his voice.

Zero just smiled. "Get in," he said.

The boys sat inside the basket and waited until a strong, wild gust of wind came straight at them. Zero pressed a button, and the very next instant, they were flying! It was so easy!

"Do you think I'm dreaming?" asked Aero.

"No," replied Zero, grinning, "only I do that!"

"Hey Zero!" shouted Aero. "I've thought of a fantastic name for our flying machine. I'm going to call it Aero-plane! What do you think?"

Zero was quiet at first.

"It would be nice to call it Zero-plane," he then said softly.

Aero was quick to agree. "Of course, Zero. It was your design. And I think your name is a better one, anyway. Thank you for making my wish come true."

"No problem," said Zero, smiling happily. "A Zero can be a Hero too, right?"

"RIGHT!" shouted Aero, as they watched the river and the boats down, down below them.

CAN I GO TO THE CIRCUS?

The circus was in town! All the children in Mintu's class were talking about it. Mintu had never, ever been to watch a circus before, but his cousin brother from Chennai had watched The Jambaroo Circus that had come all the way from Russia. He would not stop talking about the acrobats and magic tricks that he had seen.

"The Big Top was soooooo big," Raghu said. "Do you know what the Big Top is?" he had asked Mintu. Mintu shook his head. Was Raghu talking about a big spinning top?

"I told you that I have never been to a circus before," Mintu said.

"The clowns are the best!" smiled Raghu. "How I laughed and laughed! They were so funny!"

Mintu was worried. His father was away in Delhi for some important work and his mother was very busy with her office work. By the time his father would come back to Bangalore, the circus would have gone to Chennai. Mintu wanted to watch the circus so much! He waited till his mother came home that evening.

"Can we go to the circus, ma?" he asked.

"I will buy the tickets on Saturday," his mother said. "I have a holiday this Saturday.

On Saturday, Mintu rushed back after playing football in the park.

"Where are the tickets? Where are the tickets?" he shouted, pulling his mother's dupatta.

His mother hugged him but did not smile.

"I'm so sorry, Mintu," she said. "The tickets were all sold out."

Mintu was so sad.

A week went by. Almost all the children in his class had gone to watch the circus. Another week went by. By this time every child in his class had watched the circus. They would talk about nothing else during the lunch break.

"Did you see the tall clown fall of the table?" his bench mate asked Mintu on Monday.

"I have not been to the circus yet," said Mintu sadly.

On Friday, Mintu got off the school bus and Appa was standing at his bus stop! How happy he was!

All evening he chatted with his father telling about everything that happened since he had gone to Delhi, but he did not talk about the circus.

On Saturday morning, Mintu was very surprised to see his father dressed and ready by 9:00 am. He usually slept until 10:00 am on a holiday.

"Come on, Mintu," he shouted from the garage. "Your mother wants me to do some shopping. Come and help me."

So Mintu jumped into the car. His father drove out of their colony.

"You passed the super market, Appa," Mintu shouted.

"There is another one at the end of the road," his father said.

The car reached the end of the road and Mintu saw a huge, big, colourful tent in the middle of the field. He looked at his father, puzzled. His father was holding two tickets in his hand!

"Let us go to the Big Top!" Mintu's father said, ruffling his hair.

Mintu was so happy that he forgot to ask his father how he got the tickets. He had so much fun watching the acrobats and the magicians, but Raghu was right. The clowns were the best!

"Thank-you Appa," he said sleepily on the way home.

PINKY PANTHER'S PIMPLE PROBLEM

"You never bought my pimple cream," complained Pinky Panther. "I knew you would forget!"

She went puffing and panting to sulk in a corner.

"No one cares if my face is full of pimples," she muttered angrily. "I told Perky at least five times before he went shopping. But nobody ever listens to me!"

Now, Pinky Panther was fat. And Lazy. And very fond of eating. Not just her meals but also a lot of munchies in between. So, she would get tired just carrying her own weight around. And then she would huff and puff and get into a very bad mood indeed!

And every time Perky Panther teased her and pestered her to go and play with him, so that she could lose some weight, Pinky would angrier and eat a little more!

"Who does he think he is?" she would mumble angrily, as she munched and puffed away.

Perky was a very active cub and spent a lot of time with the other cubs in the neighbourhood. They'd race through the jungle at lightning speed. Pinky Panther could not understand them at all.

"Why do you waste your energy and time on such a silly activity?" she would often ask Perky.

In the beginning, Perky's answer was always the same. "I like the exercise. I need it. It's fun, Pinky. Try it." Now he no longer bothered, since Pinky wasn't willing to change.

And then, one day, there was a big fight between them. Very different from their usual arguments. They pulled each other's fur out, scratched each other's faces, and yanked each other's tails.

But Pinky Panther was at a great disadvantage because she was not used to moving fast. In fact, she wasn't used to moving much at all. Naturally, Perky Panther won, leaving poor Pinky crying.

"You are such a fat lump!" shouted Perky, as he ran off. "The only thing you move is your mouth, Pinky. You are so greedy!"

Pinky was too tired to think of something nasty to say in reply.

The fight had started over a very silly reason, as most fights do. Pinky had borrowed a book from Perky's friend Growl, and split some milk on it by mistake. Perky was very particular about how books were handled, especially those of others. He was wild with rage.

"How could you be so careless?" he had shouted. The rest of the fight merely consisted of actions.

Now, Pinky sat sulking in her cave. Her parents had not returned from work, and she was too upset to even think of eating anything.

'Perky was so mean to me,' she thought. 'I'm sure he doesn't love me at all.'

She started to cry all over again. 'In fact, I don't think anyone loves me,' she thought unhappily. 'They only nag me and call me fat and greedy.'

But, after a good bout of crying, Pinky felt much better.

"I'll show them all!" she thought firmly. "Perky thinks I only move my mouth, is it? Okay. Then I won't eat at all!"

And that's just what she did. At dinner time, when she said, "no, thank you," to the venison for the second time, Perky looked at her in shock. In fact, everyone did. But since Perky was not on talking terms with her, he didn't say a word.

Their parents didn't say anything either, though they had heard all about the fight from the neighbours. Pinky's parents never interfered in the children's fights. But they were surprised to see Pinky starving!

Meanwhile, Pinky tried to carry on as if nothing had happened. But she had to find something to do with all that time she used to spend on eating. Now, with no eating to do, Pinky was at a loss over how to keep herself occupied. So she started to do her own shopping, and even made a trip to that special shop where her pimple cream could be bought. She started walking to the library too, since she could not ask Perky (who used to collect and return her books for her before the Big Fight), and also because it was some way to spend some time at least.

Pinky knew that her parents were very keen to know what had actually made her stop eating. But she would not say a word about the Big Fight. Nor would Perky. Perky Panther now felt sorry for being so rude and nasty to his sister, but he was proud too, like Pinky was. So, neither of them was ready to apologise.

Anyway, Pinky found that she loved visiting the library so much that she almost forgot about the fight. She made a few friends there too, though the librarian became her favourite. She would suggest what books Pinky should read, and then she would discuss them with her after Pinky had read them. Without realising it, Pinky soon lost her interest in nonstop eating, and in fact, would rush through her meals so that she could finish the latest book she was reading, and go to the library again. Oh yes, she had started eating a little when her mother had got angry and finally shouted at her for starving! When her tube of pimple cream got over, Pinky didn't have the time to go and buy another one because her outings with her friends kept her so busy. Ah, Pinky had changed a lot!

What she did have time to notice, was that her clothes did not fit her anymore. They had all become quite loose. And when Perky's birthday came along, three months after the fight, she had to buy a new dress. She was busy getting ready, and wondering how she was going to wish Perky and hand over his present, when her old aunty Toto walked in.

"Who are you?" she asked Pinky, peering at her through her glasses. "You cannot be Pinky!"

"Of course I am, aunty!" exclaimed Pinky. "You need to get your glasses changed, I think!"

"Don't be cheeky, girl!" scolded Toto. "But Pinky was fat and her face was full of pimples."

Pinky ran to her mirror. And what a shock she got! Not a single pimple could she see!

"That fight was a blessing in disguise!" she shouted happily. "No over-eating, so no pimples!"

"What are you talking about, girl?" asked her aunt, puzzled.

"Nothing, nothing, dear aunty," said Pinky, giving her a hug before running out of the room.

"These young people…" muttered Toto.

Pinky found Perky admiring his volcano-shaped cake.

"Happy Birthday, big brother," she said, giving him the present.

"Thanks," aid Perky. "And I'm sorry," he whispered.

"Me too," said Pinky, hugging him.

What she did not say was that she was very grateful to him too. Thanks to him, she was a slim, sleek panther now. With no pimples. And no more pimple cream!

GRANDPA, YOU LOOK LIKE A BEET ROOT!

Grandpa never scolds me. He lets me do whatever I want. But when he is on holiday by the beach, he wants to do whatever he wants. He will not listen to anyone, not even grandma, whom everybody listens to. Nobody messes with grandma, no way!

I think grandma has given up on trying to make grandma listen when he is on holiday.

"Okay!" she says, after trying and trying to get grandpa to come indoors in the middle of the afternoon, "If you want to look like a beet root, fine! But don't complain to me later when your skin starts peeling."

Of course grandpa will complain to her when his skin starts peeling and of course grandma will say, "I told you so!" as she rubs some cool lotion on his skin. But as I said, grandpa does not listen to anybody when he is on holiday by the beach.

I always help grandpa pack for a holiday. And helping him pack for a beach holiday is the easiest. He carries the same red bag every time and as he says, "It has everything I'll need in there."

`Everything' means – 1 book, 1 towel, 1 camera, 1 Walkman, 2 bottles of water, 1 box full of munchies, 1 pair of shorts and 2 T-shirts. That's it! And poor grandma packs more clothes for him. No wonder she grumbles! He spends every single day, throughout the day, on the beach, sun bathing. He sometimes plays in the water with me, but most of the time he just chills on the beach, becoming red like a beet root every day! Grandpa really knows how to enjoy a holiday, doesn't he?

Grandparents are extra-special!

What would I do without my grandparents,
To tell me stories and pamper me?

What would I do without my grandparents,
Who never nag, and let me be?

What would I do without my grandparents,
Who give me surprise gifts when I feel sad?

What would I do without my grandparents,
Who never, ever say that I am bad?

I better remember how great they are!
I better not forget when I go far!

MONKEY TRICKS!

Don't laugh, but my pet is a monkey. Yes, a cute, tiny, lovable, funny, naughty monkey. Everyone at school laughs at me because they all have pets like dogs, cats, parrots, etc. The usual pets. So boring! My little Bubbles is so different and so much more fun to be with. Do you know why? Because he loves playing tricks on me, just like I love playing tricks on him! So, that means he is just like any other friend. Everybody says that a dog is man's best friend, but I say that a monkey can be someone's best friend too. Mine is! And my mom says that she is not sure who is naughtier – Bubbles or me! Mom loves Bubbles too, though she does get mad sometimes when Bubbles decides to snack on her lipsticks!

One morning, when I woke up, I could not find Bubbles anywhere. That was very surprising because usually Bubbles used to wake up first every day and wake me up.

'Okay, so he wants to play hide'n'seek,' I thought and started searching everywhere, but I couldn't find him. I finally got fed up of searching and since I was feeling hungry, I decided to have breakfast. Mom was still exercising so I decided to start eating my corn flakes on my own. I opened the kitchen cabinet and suddenly felt something grabbing my toe! I shouted in fright and almost dropped the box of corn flakes. Then I spotted a familiar hand. There was Bubbles hiding in the bottom cabinet! He had been waiting there just to scare me! He would have loved it if I had dropped the corn flakes box, because he loved corn flakes even more than I did!

THE PAVEMENT CLUB

There was this little boy who lived in Mumbai, by the sea. He was an only child and the only grandson of his maternal grandparents. To top it all, many of his mother's friends lived abroad. So, one thing he was never short of was toys and storybooks. He had a large room of his own with lots of shelves, absolutely full. He loved to read and listen to music. He would spend hours playing with his numerous toys.

One day, his mother was surprised when he suddenly declared, "I have too many toys!"

She wondered what he would say next.

And this is what he said. "I think I should give away some of my toys."

He wanted to give it to children who did not have much or any. He used to see many of them on the streets of Colaba. Fortunately, he met a gentleman who used to bring his dog by scooter for a walk by the sea in front of his home in Mumbai and he said he worked with poor children and was in charge of a Pavement Club.

So that is what the little boy started to do – he asked his mother for a cardboard box and every now and then he would put a toy or two into it, for the Pavement Club children. Some of the toys were slightly old, some of them were brand new. Some toys were cheap, some were expensive. When a brand new or expensive toy went into the box, in the beginning his mother would ask him if he wanted to have a re-think about giving that toy, before making a final decision But the little boy never changed his mind once he had decided. Maybe his mother was thinking about the large amount of money spent on that toy. But soon, she stopped asking. She only made sure that the toy box reached the Pavement Club children whenever it became full.

THE SUN'S ON STRIKE!

"Did you hear the latest?" whispered the Moon, looking around to see who was listening. "That silly fellow is on strike!"

"What are you talking about?" asked the tiny star, not bothering to lower his voice one bit.

"Shhhhh!" said the Moon. "Haven't you heard? It's the Sun I'm talking about. Who else would act so childish?"

"No, I had no idea," said the tiny star, looking very offended. "Nobody tells me anything around here. I am always the last one to hear the news."

"Oh, come on," said the Moon. "Don't you start sulking now. There is enough drama already. I just want to know how long that silly Sun is going to carry on like this."

In fact, that was something everyone in the whole wide Universe wanted to know.

There was so much confusion and dismay over the Sun's decision. All the world powers were having a special meeting to decide what to do about the situation. With no sunlight, the lights had to be kept on all the time. The Electricity Department in every city all over the world was thinking of ways to deal with such an unusual situation. After all, none of them had ever had to face such a strange crisis before. But the Moon, who had a very good memory, remembered something like this happening many, many years ago.

"Oh yes! The Moon exclaimed. "Don't think that I don't remember things like this. I do. My memory is better than an elephant's. And that silly Sun was quite ashamed after everything was sorted out. Just imagine! He refused to rise in the morning! Just like he's doing now."

And this was something that had happened two whole days ago. Almost 48 hours of no sunlight! Of course, the Moon and the stars got admired a lot, especially by people who normally went to sleep early on a normal day.

But since the last two days had not been normal (can YOU imagine even one day without the Sun?), people went to work, or school or wherever they would go, in the darkness. Imagine if you had to go to school at night? Wouldn't that be weird?

Rohini didn't like it one bit. "What's all this nonsense?" she grumbled. "Why can't everything go back to normal? I don't like going for nature walks. The plants look so different under the tube-lights. And I can't play any football."

Rohini's father had been reading the newspaper. He said, "It should all be fine soon, Rohini. Look, it says here that they have managed to get even Jupiter to join the talks with the Sun. And everyone knows that the Sun usually listens to Jupiter."

"I hope so," said Rohini doubtfully. "Everyone in school is saying that the Sun is just sulking. It seems; he feels that nobody appreciates him anymore and that the whole world is just taking him for granted. Is that true, Papa?"

Rohini's father smiled. "Your friends at school have been reading the newspapers! They're right. I guess this is the sun's way of making us realise how difficult it is to manage without him for even two days."

The next day (could we call it a 'day' when there was no sun?) everyone rushed for their newspapers. Everyone wanted to know whether the high-level talks had been successful. And the headlines said it all.

'SUCCESS AT LAST! Look forward to your Sun tomorrow morning!'

Rohini couldn't sleep. Most people could not. There was so much excitement in the air. Would the Sun rise? Would it not? What tension!

The Moon was wondering whether she should sulk too. "Look at all the attention that silly fellow is getting! Everyone should have just ignored him and he would have come back quietly. All this *tamasha* is going to make him feel he is sooooo important!"

"But he is," said the tiny star quietly. "The whole world has missed him so much. They all need him so much."

Rohini climbed up to her terrace. She found that every other building terrace as far as she could see was full of people. Waiting. And waiting. Facing the East…

And…when the first rays of the sun burst through the clouds, everyone started cheering…

"Three cheers for the Sun! Hip, hip, hooray! Hip, hip, hooray! Hip, hip, hooray!

THE BORED SCARECROW!

You cannot imagine what a boring life I've been leading, folks! Put yourself in my place for just ten minutes and you'll be ready to scream! Do you realise how lucky you are? To be able to move around, whenever and wherever you please? Ah, but I have no such luck. You see, I'm a scarecrow. A bored scarecrow.

Nothing happens in my part of the world. At least earlier I could see a bit of the road and the people and vehicles passing by, but now these sugar cane stalks have grown almost as tall as I am. In fact, at the rate the sugar cane is growing the stalks will soon be tickling my nose! Must be all that extra strong fertilizer that they use these days. I can barely see anything. No view at all! I wish we scarecrows had a union, so that we could fight for our rights to a view at least. Oh well, that's another dream of mine.

Oh yes, I spent a lot of time dreaming. In my job dreaming comes easy. Not much work to do, you see. I don't know what's happened to the crows these days. They've become a very lazy lot. I suspect even they go to a fast-food joint to have their meals these days! Maybe, I don't know. I've never been to a city.

In the good old days, I really had to work hard for a living. Then, the crows used to be a bold lot and I was kept busy all day, flapping my hands and scaring them away. That's what I'm for, after all. That's my job. To scare crows, right? But nowadays, a few crows fly by leisurely, and all I have to do is flap one hand calmly, and they fly away. No fighting spirit anymore. That's what the problem is.

Ouch! My joints ache! I'm not getting younger, folks. Nor is my owner. Those were the days when I'd wear a suit to work. That showed the crows that I really meant business! People used to point me out to their children when they passed by. How proud that would make me! You should have seen me then! These days nobody notices me anymore. I don't blame them though. I'm not smartly dressed anymore. Just a shabby old shirt and a tattered, old lungi.

I bet none of you have noticed me either. I'm right next to the Bangalore - Mysore Highway, in what people call the Sugar Belt. Have you? No? There, didn't I tell you I was too shabby to be noticed? My owner is too old to notice too but I'm hoping his son soon will. He lives in the city and comes here only when his two children have their holidays. Maybe they'll notice how shabby I am and get me a new set of clothes. That's another dream of mine. Don't laugh! But new clothes do make one feel great, don't they?

Yawn…it's time for my afternoon nap now. See you later…Hey! Wait a minute! What's that I see near the haystack? Sssssssh! Quietly now. Those two fellows look very suspicious. Can you believe it! They've got my master's car tires in their hands! Oh dear! What am I going to do now? Just when I was complaining that life was boring, there's daylight robbery happening right in front of my eyes! Sssssssh!

Hey, but those tyres look too small for my master's Ambassador car. That means his son must be here in his Maruti car. Where are the children then? I wish somebody would come out from the house. Everyone must be sleeping. Oh dear! Those thieves are coming this side! I've never been so scared in my whole life. Don't think I'm not brave, please? It's just that I've never had a chance to be brave. These two fellows look quite mean, you know! I hope they don't notice me shivering me with fright. What am I going to do now?

Ohh! Ohh! Ahhhhhh!

THUMP! THUD! THUMP!

'Hi friends! It's me again. Good old scarecrow. You are not going to believe what happened! As those two thieves were slinking past me with those tyres, I fainted! Yes, fainted! Right in their path! Wasn't that lucky? Those fellows tripped over me and the shock made them scream! Poor Fellows! They must have thought I was a ghost! Anyway, the next thing I know, my master's son was standing over me with two of the house servants. They must have heard the screams. They were holding the thieves very firmly. Those ruffians kept looking at poor me very suspiciously.

'If it wasn't for that old scarecrow, we'd have never been caught,' the nastier-looking one muttered.

'I see, I see,' said my owner's son, thoughtfully, as they all walked away. I kept wishing that someone would put me back in my place. It wasn't very nice lying on the ground and if any of the crows saw me, they'd never respect me anymore.

Fortunately, the two servants came back very soon. I think I saw looks of admiration in their eyes. Oh yes! I was a hero now! Any of you want my autograph? And can you believe it? I was dressed up in a suit! Just like in the old days! They even had a maroon tie for me! Wow! And when my owner's two grandchildren came out to play, you know what Harish told Seetha?

'That scarecrow is a great guy!' he said. 'He saved *appa* a lot of money.'

And both the children really looked up to me. It felt so good to be admired again! And even the crows have been coming from all over the place to see me! Oh yes, I think they must have written about me in that newspaper they have - The Crow's Voice.

So here I am, hale and hearty. I don't have much time for dreaming these days. All the crows have to be chased away. I can't have them dirtying my new suit, can I? And besides, I have to do my job well now that I'm a hero as well. I bet you've never heard of a scarecrow-hero before? Well, I'm one and I'm going to keep being one. I used to be a bored scarecrow, but now I'm a busy, happy one. Who says that dreams don't come true, huh? Look for me the next time you're travelling on the Bangalore - Mysore Highway, okay? I'll be the only scarecrow with a maroon tie! Cheerio!

RAMAN'S DREAM

Raman was still in bed, half asleep. He could hear voices and he wondered if he was still dreaming. He had had a wonderful dream about splashing in the waves at some beach that was full of shells. He had kept picking up more and more and…

No, those voices were not part of his dream. Those were the voices of his parents, and they had not been in his dream. He heard words like 'tickets' and 'suitcases' being mentioned. What was happening? Raman jumped out of bed, opened his door and ran into the dining room. But his parents were discussing the price of tomatoes! Nothing to do with tickets and suitcases. He must have been dreaming.

Anyway, he went back into his room to plan. He had to think of something to do. Most of his friends had left the city. Holidays were the time to travel, right? Raman knew that his parents could not take off from their jobs because they had used up so much of their leave when his father's mother had fallen ill in Goa. Poor *Dadima*! She would have no company this holiday, thought Raman.

'And poor me too, because I will not get pampered by her this year. And I will not get to eat the yummy *kheer* that she prepares, whenever I want.'

Raman decided to spend time on sorting out his stamp collection. It was in such a mess!

'I must finish sorting them out before school begins again,' he thought, pulling out the large toffee box in which he kept all the stamps that he had not yet arranged in their albums. 'Then I'll be able to exchange whatever duplicate stamps I have with Xerses.'

By the time he got bored with his stamps, it was time for his parents to leave for their offices.

'Bye, Raman,' said his mother. 'I'll come back early and take you for a swim.'

His father ruffled his hair and said, 'Breakfast is on the table. Bye. See you in the evening. By the way, there's something special on your plate that you will enjoy.'

Raman washed his parents through his bedroom window till they were out of sight. Maybe there are *appams* for breakfast, he hoped, as he brushed his teeth. Their old, family servant was busy washing the clothes. Raman got dressed. He was now ready for *appams*.

But was that what he got for breakfast? No!

What he saw on his plate were three sheets of paper that looked very familiar! Wow! Three tickets to Margao, Goa! Much, much better than *appams*! He couldn't wait to see his *dadima's* face! And collect all those shells!

A PASSENGER WITHOUT A TICKET!

Hozefa was reading, enjoying the rhythm that the wheels of the train made as they zipped through the tracks. His parents and older sister Tasneem were fast asleep. The family was on their way to Chennai. Hozefa was looking forward to this holiday; he was going to visit a snake farm! His father had finally promised him that, after a lot of pestering. In fact, the book he was reading was all about that snake farm.

Hozefa loved snakes. Yes, snakes. Those creepy-crawly reptiles that most people found so scary, made Hozefa so happy. He found them fascinating! He had read every book about snakes from the school library. He owned many books on snakes too. He had plastic toy snakes, soft curly pillow snakes and even a snake height chart! Anyone who stepped into Hosefa's room for the first time always got a shock! How many of you have walked into a room full of snakes? Not real ones, of course, but even large posters of them can be quite shocking, right?

Anyway, the funny thing was that Joseph had never, ever seen a real snake. He had heard of people who had a snake as a pet but when he suggested that idea to his mother, you can imagine what her reaction was! Hozefa sometimes wondered if he himself would be scared of a snake if he saw one right in front of him. His pen-pal from Assam, had a pet python. Sunjoy had just sent him a photograph of himself holding a huge 10-foot python in his hands! Hozefa had put that photograph up on his notice board.

Hozefa looked out of the window. The trains seemed to be passing a small town. He saw the lights of the station flash by. He wondered what speed the train was traveling at. His mother had told him that the engine drivers usually increased the speed of the trains at night. And then, Hozefa suddenly saw something move behind the window bars. What was that? He put his book down and leaned across to have a better look. Could it be? No way! But it did look very familiar. It did look like a …..snake! Hozefa froze! A snake!

He knew that he should wake his parents but he didn't. He watched as the long black creature moved gracefully along the bars like a trapeze artist in a circus! He could tell that it was a python. It seemed to have crawled right out of his book!

'Wait till Sunjoy hears this,' he thought.

Hozefa knew then that he was never going to be scared of these beautiful creatures. He had seen one and all he felt was respect. No fear at all! He quickly woke up his family, but the moment he did, the python disappeared.

'For your eyes only!' Tasneem teased him, when he told them what he had seen.

The Madras Crocodile Bank Trust & Centre for Herpetology

The wonderful place that Hozefa wanted his father to take him to was The Madras Crocodile Bank Trust & Centre for Herpetology. He knew that crocodile-hunting used to be a very good business a long time agoi, because of which the number of crocodiles in India had reduced a lot. So, the Indian government had protected all three species of Indian crocodilians under the Wildlife Protection Act of 1972. The Madras Crocodile Bank focused on the mugger, the saltwater crocodile and the gharial.

The bank was originally designed to be a safe place for crocodiles, to multiply until they could be returned to restock their original wild habitats.

As the need for conservation of reptiles grew, the bank increased its expertise to include turtles, lizards and snakes and it came to be known as the Madras Crocodile Bank Trust and Centre for Herpetology in 1993.

The Madras Crocodile Bank Trust and Centre for Herpetology is one of the largest reptile zoos in the world. It is spread over eight and a half acres of land. Apart from their guided tours (which Hozefa was longing to go on) the centre has a wide variety of other activities for all ages that are both informative and fun.

For outdoor lovers, there is a lot of wildlife, including large breeding colonies of water birds and a nesting beach for Olive Ridley Sea Turtles. Hozefa could hardly wait!

About the Author

Arthy Muthanna Singh

Arthy Muthanna Singh is a children's author, freelance journalist, copywriter, editor and cartoonist based in Goa. She has published over thirty-five books with publishers like Penguin Random house, Puffin, Scholastic, Tata Donnelley, Frank, Ratna Sagar, Mango Books (DC Books), etc.

She was the Senior Editor at Limca Book of Records (Coca-Cola India) for over thirteen years.

She grew up in the Nilgiris and presently lives in Goa.

Present occupation: Founder-partner/ co-author at SYLLABLES27, an independent publishing venture which produces books for children up to the age of 14 on a turn-key basis for various publishers and organizations that work with children.

Organisations that SYLLABLES27 has collaborated with include Puffin (Penguin Random House), Penguin Random House, WWF (World Wildlife Fund), Room to Read, Young INTACH, Rupa Publications, Talking Cub (Speaking Tiger), Room To Read, Om Kids, Red Panda (Westland) and Tota Books (Full Circle).

She has co-authored 28 books.

www.ingramcontent.com/pod-product-compliance
Lightning Source LLC
LaVergne TN
LVHW041557070526
838199LV00046B/2028